Disney
FROZEN
SPRINGTIME SURPRISES

PaRRagon

Bath • New York • Cologne • Melbourne • Delhi
Hong Kong • Shenzhen • Singapore

DELICIOUS DESSERTS

Anna has made tasty treats for the Winter's End Festival.
What kind of treats would you like at your party? Draw some here.

Looks yummy!

Add your reward sticker here!

SPRING IS HERE!

Sven knocked down Anna's banner for the festival. Help Olaf put the last three letters in the right place.

WE COME S RIG

P

N L

Springtime fun!

Add your reward sticker here!

Answer on page 31

3

DOT-TO-DOT DESIGNS

Elsa has created a reindeer statue for the Winter's End Festival. Connect the dots to complete the statue and color in the picture.

Add your reward sticker here!

DARLING DUCKLINGS

Olaf, Elsa, and Anna are playing in the royal gardens.
Guide mama duck through the maze and collect her ducklings
along the way.

Start

Finish

Found the right route?

Add your
reward sticker
here!

Answer on page 31

FROZEN SUNNY SEARCH

Anna and Elsa are excited about the arrival of spring.
Can you find the fun words in the grid below? Look up,
down, forward, backward, and diagonally.

Y	P	P	A	H	J	S	F
S	Z	X	B	M	U	T	L
I	P	Q	I	N	L	S	O
M	O	R	N	U	V	Q	W
V	A	Y	I	F	Y	C	E
F	Y	G	K	N	J	U	R
J	A	B	I	N	G	A	S
J	N	F	R	C	W	D	N

SPRING

FLOWER

SUNNY

HAPPY

MAGIC

Super searching!

Add your
reward sticker
here!

Answers on page 31

6

HELLO, OLAF!

Olaf is welcoming spring! Copy the picture of Olaf into the empty grid below, drawing one square at a time. Then color it in!

Awesome!

Add your reward sticker here!

FOLLOW THE FLOWERS

Anna and Elsa are collecting flowers in the garden.
Use the key below and follow the flowers to the finish.

Start

Finish

Key

Perfect!

Add your reward sticker here!

Answer on page 31

COUNTING COOKIES

Elsa and Olaf are baking cookies. Can you count how many they've made? Color in the cookies and add your answers below.

A 🍪🍪🍪🍪🍪 + 🍪🍪🍪🍪 = ☐

B 🍪🍪🍪🍪🍪🍪🍪🍪 − 🍪🍪🍪 = ☐

C 🍪🍪🍪 + 🍪🍪🍪🍪 − 🍪🍪 = ☐

Magical math!

Add your reward sticker here!

Answers on page 31

MOUNTAIN MAZE

Elsa is using her ice magic to create snow slides down the mountain.
Can you guide the sisters and Olaf back down to their castle?
Color in the flowers Olaf collected along the way!

Start

Finish

Hooray!

Add your
reward sticker
here!

10

Answer on page 31

BUSY BUMBLEBEES

Olaf is chasing bumblebees. Buzz, buzz!
How many bumblebees can you count?

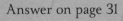
There are _____ bumblebees.

Answer on page 31

Great counting!

Add your
reward sticker
here!

11

FLORAL FUN

Olaf has decorated himself with pretty flowers.
Only two of these pictures are exactly the same.
Can you spot and circle them?

Did you spot the matching pictures?

Add your reward sticker here!

12

Answer on page 31

CHOCOLATE TREATS

Elsa and Anna are making yummy chocolate treats.
Draw your own below and add some tasty toppings.

Yummy!

Add your
reward sticker
here!

13

PERFECT PICNIC

Anna has made a picnic to share with her friends. Draw lines
to show where the missing pieces of this picture should go.

Good work!

Add your
reward sticker
here!

14

Answers on page 32

SNOWBALL FIGHT!

Anna and Elsa are having a snowball fight.
Follow the paths below and see which snowball hits Elsa.

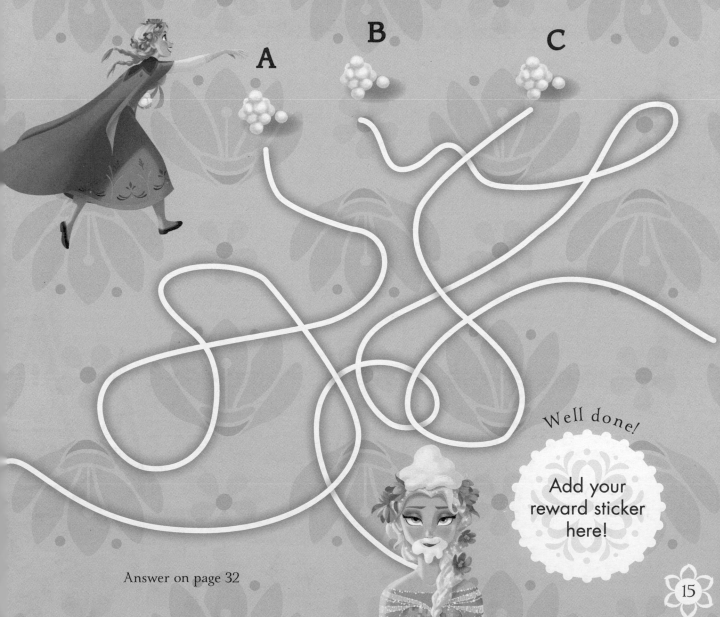

A   **B**   **C**

Well done!

Add your
reward sticker
here!

Answer on page 32

15

ICE-TASTIC PATTERNS

Anna has been skating with the children of Arendelle.
Can you draw some fun patterns on the ice?

Great drawing!

Add your
reward sticker
here!

REWARD STICKERS

© Disney

© Disney

© Disney

© Disney

© Disney

© Disney

© Disney

© Disney

© Disney

© Disney

© Disney

© Disney

© Disney

© Disney

© Disney

© Disney

JUST FOR FUN

BEAUTIFUL BUTTERFLIES

Sven loves playing with butterflies in the sunshine.
Can you draw your own butterfly below?

Lovely picture!

Add your reward sticker here!

How many little butterflies can you count on the page? _____

Answer on page 32

DAZZLING DRESS

Anna needs a new dress to wear in the spring sunshine.
Color in her dress with bright colors and add
some pretty flowers.

Beautiful!

Add your
reward sticker
here!

18

FLOWER POWER

Achoo! Kristoff has sneezed and blown Anna's flowers everywhere!
Help Kristoff arrange the flowers in the right order. There should be one
of each flower in each row and column. Use a blue, purple, orange, and
yellow crayon and draw the correct flower in each empty square
to complete the puzzle.

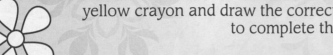

Pretty flowers!

Add your
reward sticker
here!

Answer on page 32

19

OLAF'S ADVENTURES

Olaf is dreaming about adventures in the sunshine.
Draw his dreams in the cloud below.

Nice picture!

Add your
reward sticker
here!

20

SPRINGTIME SEARCH

Olaf, Anna, and Elsa are enjoying the first dance of spring.
How many times can you find the word "spring" in the grid below?
Look down, across, and diagonally.

s	p	r	i	n	g	s	u
p	p	e	k	r	y	p	s
r	e	r	j	n	s	r	p
i	e	w	i	u	e	i	r
n	v	e	r	n	v	n	i
s	p	r	i	n	g	g	n
a	s	p	r	i	n	g	g

I can find "spring" ____ times.

Good work!

Add your
reward sticker
here!

Answer on page 32

21

SHADOW MATCH

Olaf is having fun chasing his shadow in the sunshine. Draw a line from Olaf to his matching shadow.

Great!

Add your reward sticker here!

Answer on page 32

FRIENDS AND FLOWERS

Elsa and Olaf are collecting flowers to welcome spring.
Color in the pretty picture below.

Make It Yourself!

Follow the instructions below to make your very own flower headband just like Elsa's!

You will need:
- An adult to help you.
- White craft glue (optional).

1. Gently press out the pieces of card stock at the back of the book.

2. To make the headband, connect the three long pieces by folding them along the lines and pushing the tabs through the slots. (You can glue the tabs down to make the headband more secure.)

3. You can decorate the headband by inserting the press-out flowers into each slot.

Now wear your flower headband!

Add your reward sticker here!

PRETTY PETALS

Olaf picked a petal from a flower. It looks like a heart!
Look at the pretty flowers below. Can you spot the odd one out?

A

B

C

D

E

F

Fun!

Add your
reward sticker
here!

Answer on page 32

SUNNY SAND CASTLES

Elsa and Anna are building a sand castle in the sunshine.
Draw a picture of your own magical castle here.

Cute castle!

Add your
reward sticker
here!

FUN WITH FRIENDS

Anna and Elsa have made flower garlands for their friends
Sven and Olaf. Look carefully at these two pictures.
Can you spot six differences in the picture on the right?

Color in a flower for each
difference you find.

Did you find them all?

Add your
reward sticker
here!

HIDE-AND-SEEK

Kristoff is playing hide-and-seek in the garden.
Can you guess who is hiding behind the flowers?

Did you guess who is hiding?

Add your
reward sticker
here!

Answer on page 32

OLAF'S SPRINGTIME SONG

Olaf is singing a song about his springtime adventures.
Can you add the missing words to the correct places to complete the song?

Oh, the sky will be blue and the ☐ will be shining, too.

The bees will go ☐ and kids will blow dandelion ☐.

I'll finally see a ☐ breeze blow away a winter storm

and find out what happens to solid water when it gets warm,

when I finally do what frozen things do in the sun!

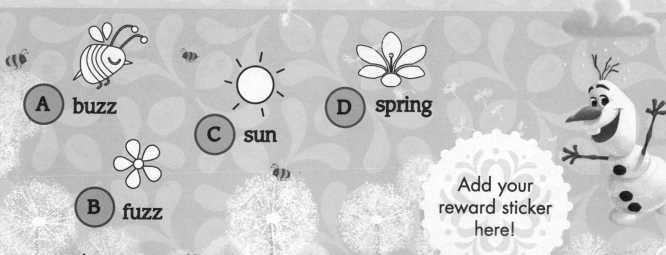

A buzz

C sun

D spring

B fuzz

Add your reward sticker here!

Answers on page 32

SPRINGTIME SISTERS

Elsa and Anna are very special sisters. They know that love can melt a frozen heart. How many of each different flower and snowflake can you count below? Write your answers in the white shapes.

Good job!

Add your reward sticker here!

Answers on page 32

ANSWERS

Page 3

Page 8

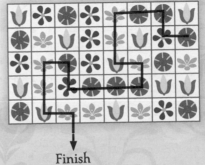

Start

Finish

Page 9

A. 9
B. 5
C. 4

Page 5

Start

Finish

Page 10

Start

Finish

Page 11
There are 11 bumblebees.

Page 6

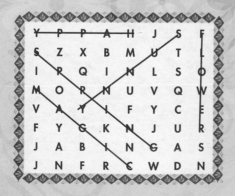

Page 12
A and E are the same.

Page 14

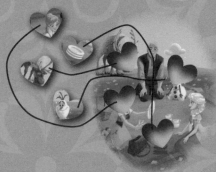

Page 15

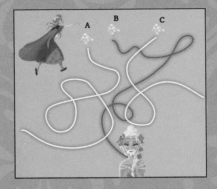

Page 17

There are six butterflies.

Page 19

Page 21

The word "spring" appears six times.

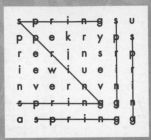

Page 22

Shadow C is the correct match.

Page 24

Flower C is the odd one out.

Page 26-27

Page 28

Sven is hiding in the garden.

Page 29

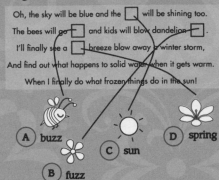

Oh, the sky will be blue and the ☐ will be shining too.

The bees will go ☐ and kids will blow dandelion ☐.

I'll finally see a ☐ breeze blow away a winter storm,

And find out what happens to solid water when it gets warm.

When I finally do what frozen things do in the sun!

A buzz

B fuzz

C sun

D spring

Page 30

3   5   4   2

32